# A Merry Bunny Christmas

## Grosset & Dunlap

Based upon the animated series *Max & Ruby*
A Nelvana Limited production © 2002–2003.

Library of Congress Control Number: 2009017619

ISBN 978-0-448-45228-9          10 9 8 7 6 5 4 3

"Max, it is almost Christmastime. We should decorate our tree," said Max's sister, Ruby. "Let's see what's in the ornament box!"

Max wheeled over his wagon. It was filled with toys.
"Decorate!" said Max.
"No, Max. Toys don't go on the tree," said Ruby. "We have to use real Christmas ornaments."

Ruby hung a long popcorn chain on the tree.

Max hung a long boa constrictor snake.
"No toys on the tree, Max," said Ruby.

7

"Look! My favorite golden horn!" shouted Ruby. "And my favorite gingerbread man, too!"

Max thought the gingerbread man looked yummy.
He hung a pair of vampire fangs on the tree.
"Gross!" said Ruby.

"My ornaments are so pretty," said Ruby. "Look at this sweet reindeer and these shiny icicles!"

Max thought his red, spotted bug and outer space robot were just as nice.

"Oh, Max . . ." said Ruby.

"Look at this wonderful snowflake, Max!" said Ruby.

Max hung up a tarantula and a spiderweb.

"All done!" said Ruby, gazing proudly at the tree.
"Oh no, Max! I forgot the star!"

Ruby tried to put the star on the tree. But she could not reach.

"We should have hung the star first! If we try to hang it now, the other ornaments might break," said Ruby.

Max had an idea.
He flew his Disaster Rescue Helicopter right out of his wagon.

He hooked a sparkling pinwheel to the helicopter.
Then he flew the helicopter up, up, up!

Max's pinwheel landed right on the tippy-top of the Christmas tree.

"Decorate!" said Max.

"Wow, Max! It looks just like a real star!" said Ruby.

"I guess toys can go on the tree after all."

**Merry Christmas from Max & Ruby!**